SUPER FLY

Super Fly vs.
Furious Flea!

The Super Fly series

The World's Smallest Superhero!

Revenge of the Roach!

Super Fly vs. Furious Flea!

Rise of the Evil Army!
(coming soon)

Super Fly vs. Furious Flea!

Todd H. Doodler

BLOOMSBURY
NEW YORK LONDON OXFORD NEW DELHI SYDNEY

To my favorite little fly on the wall, Elle

First published in the United States of America in October 2016
by Bloomsbury Children's Books
www.bloomsbury.com

Bloomsbury is a registered trademark of Bloomsbury Publishing Plc

For information about permission to reproduce selections from this book, write to
Permissions, Bloomsbury Children's Books, 1385 Broadway, New York, New York 10018
Bloomsbury books may be purchased for business or promotional use. For information on
bulk purchases please contact Macmillan Corporate and Premium Sales Department at
specialmarkets@macmillan.com

Library of Congress Cataloging-in-Publication Data
Names: Doodler, Todd H., author.
Title: Super Fly vs. Furious Flea! / by Todd H. Doodler.
Description: New York : Bloomsbury USA Children's, 2016. | Series: Super Fly! ; 3
Summary: Super Fly and Fantastic Flea have always fought the bad guys together,
but Crazy Cockroach's latest plan to take over the world involves turning
Super Fly's loyal sidekick, Fantastic Flea, against him.
Identifiers: LCCN 2015046653 (print) | LCCN 2016022994 (ebook)
ISBN 978-1-61963-384-1 (paperback) • ISBN 978-1-61963-385-8 (hardcover)
ISBN 978-1-61963-386-5 (e-book)
Subjects: | CYAC: Superheroes—Fiction. | Flies—Fiction. | Fleas—Fiction. | Insects—Fiction. |
BISAC: JUVENILE FICTION / Humorous Stories. | JUVENILE FICTION / Action & Adventure /
General. | JUVENILE FICTION / Comics & Graphic Novels / Superheroes.
Classification: LCC PZ7.D7247 Suf 2016 (print) | LCC PZ7.D7247 (e-book) | DDC [Fic]—dc23
LC record available at https://lccn.loc.gov/2015046653

Book design by Nicole Gastonguay and Yelena Safronova
Printed and bound in the U.S.A. by Berryville Graphics Inc., Berryville, Virginia
2 4 6 8 10 9 7 5 3 1 (paperback)
2 4 6 8 10 9 7 5 3 1 (hardcover)

All papers used by Bloomsbury Publishing, Inc., are natural, recyclable products
made from wood grown in well-managed forests. The manufacturing processes
conform to the environmental regulations of the country of origin.

CONTENTS

1

A Fly and His Pie

Brown Barge Elementary School floated inside a broken toilet at the center of Stinkopolis's city dump. It was the only all-bug school of its kind in the area. Classes began in September, at the end of the busy pollinating, stinging, and sweat-licking season known to humans as summer. School ended with the first frost, when most of Stinkopolis hibernated or flew south.

Amazingly, just a few short weeks after his first miserable day at Brown Barge,

fourth grader Eugene Flystein found himself being named Student of the Season for
all his hard work, and for saving the whole

school from turning
into zombies. Of
course, they didn't
realize that it wasn't
Eugene who had
saved them.

If you recall, in six seconds Eugene
became 9,000 times smarter—and stronger, faster, and just plain super! Becoming
Super Fly was the power of Eugene's greatest invention to date: the patented piece of
key lime pie called the Ultimo 6-9000.

Don't bother looking for it in the local
bakery, your favorite restaurant, or the gro-
cery store. Not even the Internet offers real
live superhero supplies (yet). The remains
of that powerful pastry can only be found in
one place—the Flysteins' fridge.

Before the first day of school, Eugene had no idea if the Ultimo 6-9000—disguised as a delicious piece of pie—

would work. Then again, most of his inventions didn't work. That was the really annoying thing about being an inventor.

But within six seconds, Eugene felt a surge of energy, a burst of awesomeness, and an explosion of power! Before eating the pie, Eugene had been an ordinary fly. Actually, a pretty clumsy, nonathletic, and nerdy specimen. Okay, he was a fly who could barely fly!

Then suddenly Eugene could fly to the moon and back in less time than it used to take him to get from the Flystein home to the Poopermarket! On that day, Eugene became Super Fly, the tiny superhero who saved Stinkopolis and the rest of the world from Crazy Cockroach!

When Eugene's adoring little sister, Elle, later helped herself to some of that patented pie, she became 9,000 times better in just six seconds too. (Seriously, it's totally patented, so don't even think about trying to duplicate the formula.)

With the addition of a *fly* costume (pun intended) and a nifty name, the second grader began her career as the stylish superhero known as Fly Girl.

Eugene expected his pest friend, Fred Flea, to try the pie. But on that fateful first day of school Fred refused to taste the tart, lime-flavored dessert of destiny. Instead, he opted to remain only as "fantastic" as his natural flea physique and the training for the family circus made him.

Fred preferred to be Super Fly's sidekick, Fantastic Flea. Even without superpowers,  Fred played a crucial part in Super Fly's ongoing battles against Crazy Cockroach. It was David vs. Goliath. Good vs. evil. Fly and Flea vs. Roach.

The evil cockroach had also been enhanced 9,000 times by the super snack. To most of Brown Barge Elementary, he was known only as that annoying bully Cornelius C. Roach.

Students knew Cornelius stole their lunch money, tripped them in the halls, and pulled their wings or antennae until they begged for mercy. But they had no idea that in his secret identity he'd once nearly taken over the world with a robot army, and then again with a hideously hypnotic video game.

Nor did those innocent insects know that the fate of Stinkopolis, and every other place on earth, had recently been decided by a Ping-Pong match between the ruthless super villain and the Super Fly who invented that super pie.

The match took place in the villain's luxurious lair, located in one side of a dirty diaper. The other side housed the headquarters of the heroes: Super Fly, Fly Girl, and their loyal, leaping sidekick, Fantastic Flea. The heroes' side of the diaper didn't even  have a mini refrigerator or a big-screen TV, much less a Ping-Pong table. (Kind of a sore point with all of them.)

The match between the super roach and mega fly didn't last long. The Ping-Pong ball flew faster than a runaway comet! When the wind died down, Super Fly was victorious.

If the villain had honored his promise, the conflict for full possession of the dirty diaper and for peace on earth would've ended then and there. But villains never keep promises, especially when they have their fingers crossed and swear to have their revenge and never stop trying to take over the world. And that's exactly what Crazy Cockroach did!

2

It's a Wonderful Life

Being named Student of the Season meant a lot to Eugene Flystein, and especially to his parents and sister, who couldn't have been prouder. Remember, his exploits as Super Fly were secret, and he didn't exactly have a zillion sports trophies on his

shelves. Nerdy, eyeglasses-wearing Eugene had books instead. Oh, and one spelling bee second-place ribbon from when he lost to Belinda Bee. (It's pretty hard to beat a bee in a spelling bee contest.)

Eugene framed the page of the *Stinkopolis Grimes* reporting on the award. He hung it on the cottony-soft absorbent wall in the Fortress of Doody (the heroes' side of the diaper). Eugene liked the caption: Brown Barge Elementary School's Super Student, Eugene Flystein.

He always chuckled to himself, thinking, "If the rest of Stinkopolis only knew how super I really am!"

Of course, for the safety of the Flystein family and friends like Fred Flea, Eugene never revealed his superpowers in public. Still, being Student of the Season was almost as good.

Everybug seemed to know him—even teachers and sixth graders. Girl bugs, like the lovely Lucy Kaboosie, suddenly noticed Eugene more. Did the sun shine brighter? Did the poo-poo platter actually taste even poo-ier?

Maybe everything was the same, but Eugene felt different. He felt like a Big Bug on Campus, a cool dude, an insect of respect.

When Eugene strutted down the halls of Brown Barge Elementary, everybug waved a leg or wing or at least tipped an antenna.

Fred Flea was impressed. "Wow! That was the captain of the bugball team!"

Eugene shrugged. If he dared to use his powers in public he would win every sport!

"Hi, Eugene!" Lucy Kaboosie fluttered her spotted wing covers.

Eugene thought she was the most beautiful ladybug he'd ever seen. He pushed up his eyeglasses and blinked at the vision of Lucy waving above her books. "Um . . . yeah . . . hi! Hi, Lucy!" Apparently being super was no help when it came to talking to pretty girls.

Just then a Ping-Pong ball sailed in front of Eugene's face. The fly turned to see two sixth graders tapping a ball between paddles as they walked down the hall.

Fred shook his head. "This is getting ridiculous!"

The flea was right. Every bug at Brown Barge had gone Ping-Pong crazy! By beating Crazy Cockroach, Super Fly had created a Ping-Pong epidemic! Every flat surface was turned into a Ping-Pong table. Desks, counters, even the backs of some of the bigger beetles.

The halls echoed with the rhythmic *pa-ping, pa-pong* of the small white balls bouncing and flying, landing and rolling.

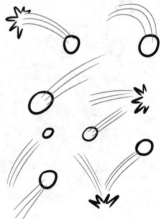

Eugene loved the game. But even he

agreed with Fred. "Playing in the halls is a bit much."

As he spoke another ball zipped right past Eugene's wings to slap Fred in the face! The student who swatted the ball quickly apologized. "Eugene Flystein! So sorry! I didn't mean to hit you."

"No harm," Eugene said.

"Some harm!" Fred protested, rubbing his sore face.

But no one noticed. Fred slumped miserably. Something was different. The Student of the Season wasn't interested in Fred anymore. Eugene never wanted to hang out and play video games, like he felt too important for his own pest friend.

Fred wanted to ask Elle about this. But the second grader had become something of a Big Bug on Campus herself.

After all, her only brother had been named Student of the Season. And even though Elle's superpowers were also a carefully guarded secret, being 9,000 times faster, stronger, and smarter had given the girl a megadose of self-confidence.

Fred told himself, "I should be happy for my friends." But he didn't feel happy. Fred felt as useless as a dented Ping-Pong ball.

3

Home Alone

Unlike his pest friend, Eugene felt more important than ever. The Student of the Season had been chosen president of the Math Club, the Science Club, the Geology Club, the Waste Management Club, and the Cooking with Poo Club.

If no one was looking, Eugene sometimes resorted to flying at super speed between club meetings. Just to keep his superpowers from getting rusty.

Fred was busy after school too. Lately he'd been spending more time training with his family. Fred hoped to  learn enough flea circus tricks to join the family business one day.

It was fine that the two bug buddies were pursuing separate interests. But it didn't exactly feel like they were pest friends anymore.

That's why Fred was so excited a few days later on the bus ride home when Eugene suggested, "Let's play *Sewer Invaders* today."

Fred grinned. "Sounds great! We can pig out on junk food and see if we can make it past level two."

Eugene smiled back. "Yeah, it's about time we took on those albino alligators."

Fred added, "Mom just bought a big box of those new bite-size scabs."

Eugene rubbed his stomach eagerly. "Your house it is! I'll get there around four."

"See you then!" Fred agreed as the friends got off the bus. Then, after a quick high-flyve tap with Eugene and a cheery wave to Elle, the athletic flea happily leaped toward his home on Compost Drive.

Fred rushed through his homework and chores. He wanted to be ready for Eugene's arrival.

Fred took the big box of snack-size scabs out of the pantry. He looked at the clock. It was only a quarter to four. He was anxious for Eugene to arrive. It'd been a while

SCABS

NEW!

IMPROVED!

NOW WITH MORE PUS!

since they shared some quality bug time together.

Fred felt tempted to open the box and taste one of the "new!" "improved!" "now with more pus!" scabs. But he decided to wait for Eugene, maybe even until after their first game. This was going to be awesome!

Fred watched seconds tick by on the Flea family clock. He tried doing math in his head like Eugene. Sixty seconds in a minute. Fifteen minutes till four o'clock . . .

Fred's brain rebelled. He'd already done his homework. This was fun time!

Fred practiced somersaults. So as the clock slowly tick-tocked, Fred leaped and twirled, spun and jumped.

Meanwhile, in the Flystein kitchen, Elle and several of her little friends were playing board games.

"Don't you want to play *Shoots and Sewers* too?" asked little Penny Pillbug.

Eugene chuckled warmly. "Thanks anyway. But I'm too busy for games."

Elle stared at Eugene. "Weren't you going to play video games with Fred today?"

Eugene glanced at the clock. He could still make it to Fred's (especially if no one was looking and he could fly at super speed). But Eugene was making some real progress on the equations for the next math team practice and he wanted to wait for the results on this latest tweak to that elusive invisibility formula . . .

Eugene realized that Elle was still staring at him. He murmured, "Kinda busy. Fred'll understand."

Elle felt troubled. Eugene was usually so thoughtful. Didn't he realize Fred was waiting for him? Didn't Eugene care?

Her brother accepted a plate of moldy cheese Poopritos offered by one of Elle's other friends. "Thank you!"

The tiny moth burst into giggles. Her fuzzy antennae jiggled with excitement.

Elle started to ask, "Shouldn't you at least call Fred?"

But Eugene was already walking back to his room.

Eugene had been so quick to say, "Fred will understand." But would he? Elle didn't!

This was no way for her kind, sweet brother to treat anybug, much less his pest friend.

Back at the Flea home, Fred heard the door-bell ring. He rushed the landing on his triple somersault and nearly bit his own foot!

"I'll be right there!" Fred shouted as he raced to the door.

Fred flung it open, expecting Eugene. Instead, a burly moving beetle announced, "Delivery for 24 Compost Drive."

Disappointment washed over Fred. "That's across the street," he told the beetle.

House number 24 had been empty ever since the Silverfish family had moved to an apartment in nearby Draintown Abbey.

"Thanks, kid," the gruff beetle grumbled, hurrying to tell his crew their mistake.

Fred looked across the street at the empty house. He wondered who his new neighbors were. Did they have any school-age pupae, maybe even someone in fourth grade?

Fred wanted to share this enormous news with Eugene. Where was he? Fred looked at the clock. It was almost six!

Suddenly, he felt worried. What if Crazy Cockroach had attacked Super Fly? After all, the villain had sworn revenge and demanded a Ping-Pong rematch! Perhaps poor Eugene had been jumped on his way to Compost Drive?

Picking up the phone, Fred frantically dialed the Flysteins' number.

4

Walking Tall

After only one ring, Elle answered.

Fred asked, "Is Eugene there?"

Elle didn't say, "Oh no! He left for your house two hours ago!"

She simply shouted, "Eugene! Fred's on the phone."

After a few minutes, Fred heard his friend's voice. "Oh, hi, Fred."

Eugene sounded distracted.

"What's going on?" Fred asked.

"Just working. I might actually have

solved part of the invisibility problem," Eugene began. "It's not that the particles aren't stable; it's the mixture . . ."

Fred felt a rush of anger—and hunger. "Do you know what time it is?"

Eugene restricted his clock-watching to the classroom. When he worked on his inventions, time didn't exist.

Fred answered for him. "It's almost six."

Fred's stomach growled. Soon it would be suppertime—and he hadn't even eaten his after-school snack.

It would serve Eugene right if Fred ate all the snack-size scabs. But he suddenly felt more sad than hungry.

"You . . . were just inventing stuff?" Fred

stammered. "You're always inventing stuff. Why didn't you at least ask me to help?"

Eugene usually loved showing off his inventions to Fred. Sometimes just by looking at them and asking questions Fred helped Eugene solve a pesky problem.

Eugene didn't notice Fred's distress. He simply felt eager to get back to work. "Yeah. I'm sorry I forgot about going to your house today. We should totally do that another time."

Fred didn't bother answering. He didn't even say good-bye. He just hung up!

Eugene shrugged and returned to his room.

Fred was angry! He jumped so high and so fast that he bounced off the ceiling and ricocheted off the walls before he finally landed in the middle of the living room.

"I don't need friends who don't appreciate me," Fred fumed. "I can go it alone. Who needs any other bugs? Not me! I'm an independent parasite. I'll just focus on being the best flea I can be."

Fred flipped over and over, executing a perfect landing before raising two legs in the air like a gymnast in the Bug Olympics.

"I'll be awesome!" Fred told himself. "I don't need to ride on anyone else's wings. I'm my own bug."

Talking out loud made Fred feel even lonelier. So he added defiantly, "Who needs enemies when you have friends like Eugene?" Then he muttered, "So what if he is Super Fly? I'm Fantastic Flea, and that's a pretty big deal too!"

Fred squared his shoulders and stood

up straighter. "I'm nobody's sidekick any-more. I may be just a flea, but I'm walking tall from now on."

After dinner, instead of relaxing in front of the TV, Fred decided to do more practicing. He asked his father to spot him as he tried some of the family's more difficult tricks.

Mr. Flea applauded. "You're really taking it to the next level."

Fred took an extra-deep bow. Every muscle ached with fatigue. But Fred was smiling. He felt determined to be the best flea in the world!

The next day, Fred acted as if Eugene Flystein didn't exist. Instead of chatting on the bus, Fred sat in the back and buried his face in a book.

He heard Eugene's friendly "Hello." Fred just didn't respond. He even ignored Elle.

During lunch, Fred devoured his blood sausage sandwich before Eugene even came off the line with his tray. Then Fred rushed off to the gym to do some stretches before his next class.

Fred savored his father's praise of "taking it to the next level." He bent deeper into the stretch and thought, "You bet I am. I'm one fantastic flea!"

Eugene spent yet another busy Friday as Brown Barge's Student of the Season. Everywhere he went bugs wanted him for something.

Did Eugene know the math answers? What were his plans for the weekend? Had he found out about the

Chess Club field trip yet? Had he tried the new poopsicles in the cafeteria yet?

Questions and greetings bounced around Eugene as fast as the Ping-Pong balls bouncing all over the halls. Yet he felt bothered by the strange sensation that something was missing.

Eugene didn't even know what until he and Elle were riding the bus back home. Elle asked, "How's Fred?"

Eugene blinked.

A Ping-Pong ball flew past his eyeglasses.

Elle started to repeat her question, but Eugene interrupted her. "I know what you asked. I just don't know the answer." Then he explained, "I haven't spoken to Fred all day!"

Elle looked alarmed. "When was the last time that happened?"

Eugene's super-enhanced memory swiftly recalled every one of his days at Brown Barge Elementary School—from that fateful first day when he met Fred to this.

Elle answered her own question before Eugene did. She said, "Never."

Eugene suggested, "Maybe he went home sick or something."

Elle shook her head. She'd seen Fred several times, but he'd always been too far away to hear her voice. Eugene recalled seeing Fred walking fast, with a purpose, standing tall—and not the least bit interested in his pest friend.

Eugene sighed. "That's weird."

Elle echoed, "Very."

The Flysteins were so busy puzzling over Fred's strange behavior that they failed to notice the big bug sitting behind them. Cornelius C. Roach found their conversation extremely interesting.

The roach lived in an agony of anger, flinching at every Ping-Pong ball flying by and every paddle's slap because they reminded him of his defeat by Super Fly.

Cornelius rubbed his forefeet with evil glee. So Fantastic Flea and Super Fly were on the outs . . . Crazy Cockroach's

9,000-times-enhanced brain processed this exciting data.

A Ping-Pong ball sailed past the bully. Without thinking, Cornelius seized the annoying sphere and crushed it into powder finer than pollen.

As Andy Ant and his friend Ted Tarantula puzzled over  their missing ball, a new plan for revenge reared its ugly head—an ugly roach head!

About Fiona

Saturday morning seemed like a good time to meet the new neighbors. So Fred strolled across Compost Drive with some poodle-blood pudding his mother had made.

He knocked on the door. As he waited, the suspense grew. Would the neighbors be nice? Would there be any bugs Fred's age? Would they like poodle-blood pudding? Fred wouldn't mind taking the delicious dessert back home.

Then suddenly the door flew open to

reveal . . . one of the prettiest young fleas
Fred had ever seen! She said, "Hi."

Fred replied, "Hi."

Then came an awkward silence. After
which both Fred and the pretty flea started
talking at the same time.

Both stopped, started again, and then
burst out laughing. When their giggles died
down, Fred said, "Welcome to Stinkopolis."

The girl said, "Thanks. I'm Fiona."

"I'm Fred Flea—and this is my mom's poodle-blood pudding. I hope you like it," Fred replied.

Fiona squealed. "Poodle pudding's my favorite!"

"Mine too!" Fred exclaimed.

"Why don't you come inside and have some?" Fiona offered.

Soon Fred was sharing pudding with Fiona and the rest of the Biteswell clan, even though he'd already sneaked some while waiting outside. Fred tried to remember the names of all of Fiona's fifty-seven brothers and sisters. But mostly he just enjoyed being the center of attention.

Fiona laughed at all of Fred's jokes. She thought his circus tricks were amazing.

"We should hang out sometime," Fiona suggested.

Fred smiled. "What about now? I can show you the neighborhood."

Fiona told her mother, "I'll do my chores later."

Then she ran out the door before Mrs. Biteswell could respond.

Since Fred had already done his chores, his mother didn't mind him going to the park with the new neighbor.

A few minutes later, Eugene knocked on the Flea family's door.

"I'm sorry, Eugene. Fred just went out with another friend," Mrs. Flea said.

"Will you tell him I stopped by?" Eugene asked.

Mrs. Flea agreed, but she hadn't felt like

herself since she'd bitten a sick hamster. By the time Fred came home, she'd forgotten all about Eugene's visit.

On his way back to Rumbling Rock Road, Eugene told himself he didn't care. He had better things to do than chase Fred. Eugene could play *Sewer Invaders* by himself. And wouldn't Fred be mad if Eugene made it to level three on his own?

For the first time in weeks, Fred wasn't thinking about Eugene at all. He was too busy looking for a neighborhood dog to ride with Fiona.

Eugene didn't even like dogs much, just their droppings. But as a fellow flea, Fiona understood the wonder of canines. One common animal combined swift transportation, comfort, warmth, and a tasty meal! No wonder dogs were considered a flea's best friend. Or is it meal?

Fred sighed. "I'm sorry there aren't any dogs around this morning."

Fiona shrugged. "That's okay. I'm still full from all that yummy poodle-blood pudding."

Fred smiled. He liked this girl! Fiona was fun and easygoing.

Then he saw a large figure coming toward them. Two smaller bugs flanked the bigger one. Fred knew that treacherous trio. His heart pounded with dread.

Cornelius C. Roach wasn't just the

meanest bully at Brown Barge Elementary School. He was, of course, also the super villain Crazy Cockroach! And his henchbugs, Dee and Doo Dung, weren't exactly Bug Scouts either.

Would these boys cause trouble for Fred and his new friend? Fred braced for a possible attack.

Instead, he heard a friendly, "Hello, Fred!"

Had Cornelius actually called Fred by his correct name?

Then Cornelius said, "Want to play a game? Five spiders from Grungeberg just challenged us to some bugball."

Fred loved bugball, but how could he play with his and Super Fly's mortal enemy? Before Fred could frame a proper refusal, Fiona said, "Sure!"

The next thing Fred knew he was playing bugball— and having a great time! Eugene never wanted to play bugball. But Fiona seemed to love the game as much as Fred did. Even when the spiders started cheating by throwing silk, she stayed right on the ball. When they weren't tripping over each other, Dee and Doo were pretty good players too. Add in the fact that Cornelius was

9,000 times stronger than a normal cockroach and it's easy to understand why their team won.

"That was fun!" Fiona declared.

Fred agreed. "Totally!" He hadn't enjoyed himself that much since the opening night of his family's flea circus.

Then the shock set in. Had Fred really just played a fun game with . . . Cornelius and the nasty Dung twins? Was he dreaming? Was he in a food coma from eating too much pudding?

"We should play again sometime soon," Cornelius suggested.

Across the playing field Elle spotted her brother's pest friend talking to his worst enemy, his henchbugs Number 1 and Number 2, and a girl she didn't recognize. Using her 9,000-times-enhanced hearing, Elle heard Fred say, "Um, yeah, let's do this again, I guess."

"Cool," Cornelius concluded. "Catch you later, buddy!"

As Cornelius and the twins walked away, Elle heard Fred remark to Fiona, "This is so weird! Cornelius and the Dungs used to bully me and my friend Eugene."

"Really? He seemed so nice," Fiona said. Then she added, "Where's Eugene?"

Fred didn't know—and he was trying very hard not to care.

Then someone tapped Fred on the shoulder. He turned around, hoping to see Eugene. But it was Cornelius!

The big roach smiled as he handed Fred the bugball. "Game ball, Fred. You earned it!"

Fred held the ball and muttered, "Thanks."

He felt almost too confused to speak. Once Cornelius was out of normal hearing range, Fred whispered, "So I guess Cornelius and I are friends now?"

Fiona grinned. "Sure looks like it! He did call you 'buddy!'"

The roach with the 9,000-times-enhanced hearing also smiled. This was all part of his plan! *Bwa-ha-ha-ha-ha!*

6

Thelma and Louise

That evening Fred's aunts, Thelma and Louise Flea, came for dinner. The last time they'd visited, Eugene had been with Fred. So Thelma asked, "How is that fly friend of yours?"

Louise added, "The nerdy one with the eyeglasses. What was his name?"

"Eugene," Fred said. "He's fine—Student of the Season at Brown Barge Elementary, in fact. But we haven't been hanging out as much lately."

"That's good," Thelma declared. "I mean, you shouldn't be spending so much time with a fly."

Louise bristled. "I thought Eugene was a nice, bright kid, if shy. There's nothing wrong with flies. Some of my best friends are flies."

"Name one," Thelma challenged.

"Buzz Flywheel, Buzzy Stenchhopper, and Flyette Garbageberg," Louise answered.

Thelma was skeptical. "Oh, please. You haven't seen them since we stopped going to the Steaming Pile Club in Kenneltown ages ago."

Louise argued, "Friends are friends whether you're with them all the time or not."

Fred wondered. Wasn't a big part of friendship hanging out together?

"Fred shouldn't have one pest friend anyway," Thelma stated. "It's better to have lots of friends than just one. Not safe to take all your bites from one dog."

Just then the doorbell rang. Fred raced to answer, hoping to see Eugene. Instead, he found Fiona.

Since the Fleas had finished dinner, Fred went outside to play with her. As they left, Fred heard Thelma tell Louise, "Fiona's a much better friend for Fred."

Meanwhile, at the Flystein home, Elle knocked on her brother's door.

"Come in," Eugene grunted.

The corner of the room that served as

Eugene's lab was a mess. He sighed. "I got frustrated with the invisibility formula, so I went back to the problem robot. And it's still a problem!"

Elle suggested, "Maybe Fred could help."
Eugene smiled. "Good idea! I'll call Fred."
It'd be nice to hang out with his good buddy

again. Maybe Eugene had been working too hard.

Mrs. Flea answered the phone. "Fred's outside playing with his new friend. Should I call him in?"

Eugene said, "No." He didn't want to interrupt a game. He told himself he wasn't jealous. He almost believed that. "Please tell him I called. Bye."

Elle studied her brother's unhappy face. "Why don't you join Fred and his new friends?"

Eugene shook his head. "I should really get this work done. The world needs a robot that can tie shoelaces."

Fred was having a great time playing kick the can with Fiona when Cornelius and the Dung twins came down Compost Drive. Fred tensed at their approach. Game ball or not, he still wasn't used to thinking of the bully as a pal.

Before Fred could even begin to invent an excuse, Fiona agreed to let Cornelius and the twins join their game.

Once again, Fred found himself having

fun with his former foe. Between Fred's natural speed and Cornelius's 9,000-times-enhanced abilities they enjoyed quite a game!

Cornelius got so excited he kicked the can into orbit. "Oops! Guess we'll have to find another can," he exclaimed, adding, "Or we could sneak into a movie."

Fiona shouted, "**YES!** I'm dying to see *Fart Wars*."

"We are too!" the Dungs declared in unison. "Fart Vader is our idol!"

Fred had never sneaked into a movie before. He wanted to say, "We should buy tickets." But he didn't want to seem like a party pooper. Besides, if the others couldn't pay, then maybe this fun evening would end. So Fred said, "Let's go!"

He followed Cornelius and the Dungs through a tiny side entrance that said Employees Only. An usher saw Fiona, but she ran so fast they didn't get caught.

Fiona giggled. Fred did too.

She said, "That was awesome!"

Fred had to agree. "Totally awesome!" He was beginning to suspect that being bad was . . . fun!

Fred thought back on all the time he and Eugene had spent trying so hard to become heroes. Maybe they'd had it all wrong. Maybe Fred should just kick back and be a kid sometimes.

Then the movie began: *May the Farts be with you* . . .

7

Furious Flea

All Sunday Eugene thought about calling Fred, but he felt funny about it. What if Fred really was trying to avoid him?

Fred considered calling Eugene. Then he remembered the long, hungry afternoon of waiting when Eugene didn't show up—or even call.

So the pest friends didn't communicate until Eugene saw Fred at school Monday morning.

"Hello, Fred!" Eugene said.

Fred shrugged.

"Where've you been lately?" Eugene asked.

"I've been around—if you'd bother to look." Fred added, "I have new friends."

Eugene felt hurt. "So I've heard. Your neighbor . . ."

"Fiona," Fred supplied the name. "And Cornelius and the Dungs too!" the flea exclaimed defiantly.

Eugene had never seen Fred so angry before, not even the time Eugene hogged all the double-stuffed scabs. "Why are you so furious?"

"Furious," Fred mused. "That's a cool name." He walked away, leaving Eugene completely puzzled.

After school, Fred didn't stop by the

Fortress of Doody. He went to the other side of the diaper, the evil side.

Fred told Cornelius, "Let's have fun, make trouble, and get into some mischief."

The cockroach could hardly believe his ears.

"Are you feeling okay?" asked the nefarious roach.

Fred explained, "I've had enough of trying to be Fantastic with Mr. President-of-Everything Super Nerd. My new name is Furious—Furious Flea."

Lucy Kaboosie Tries to Make a Trucie

The next day at school, Lucy Kaboosie cornered Fred in the cafeteria. "Since we're all friends, I thought I could talk to you on Eugene's behalf."

Fred yawned. He, Cornelius, the Dungs, and Fiona had spent a wild night on the loose in Stinkopolis.

Lucy went on, "You're too nice a bug to hang out with the bully crew."

Fred continued to look bored.

"You can't trust those guys!" Lucy exclaimed. "This is probably some kind of trap."

Just then, Fiona put down her tray next to Fred's lunch. Fiona took one look at the pretty ladybug and said, "You should probably bug off."

As the daughter of Stinkopolis's mayor and one of the most popular bugs at Brown Barge, Lucy wasn't used to being talked to that way. She turned her spotted back on Fiona and marched off in a huff. But not before getting in an insult of her own.

"Bite me!" said Lucy.

"That's what we fleas do best!" smirked Fiona.

Fred burst out laughing. He'd never had two pretty girls fight over him before.

Lucy didn't go back to her usual table. Instead, she found Elle at a table full of

giggling second graders. Lucy pulled Elle aside and whispered, "Fred's gone bad!"

"He wouldn't!" Elle exclaimed.

Lucy described her talk with Fred and Fiona, concluding, "Those fleas are after your brother. See for yourself."

Elle used her superpowers to both see and hear whatever she could from Fred's table. Fred told old jokes, and Fiona laughed her head off.

Elle wondered if she should go over there. But what would she say? Fiona seemed loud and a bit flashy, but was she really bad? More important, was Fred really being bad, or had he just decided not to bother with the Flysteins anymore?

Elle got her answer that night while she

and Eugene watched the news. The lead story began, "Stinkopolis reeks with crime this evening as reports of vandalism and theft swamp the police station."

Eugene and Elle's super senses tingled as Alexander Aphid reported live from Dog Poop Park. "As you can see, all the benches have been stacked in a giant pyramid. Police are baffled by this pointless act of vandalism. Who could've moved so many benches so quickly? So far, no witnesses have come forward.

"In a possibly related incident, every candy store in Stinkopolis has been robbed, and a giant blob of bubble gum had to be removed from the entrance to Brown Barge Elementary School."

Elle stared at the city's finest peeling a sticky pink patch off the school's double front door. "Ew!"

The earnest Aphid went on. "Candy wrappers have been found on every street in Stinkopolis. So far the only clue police have is this surveillance footage taken from outside the Doo Drop Inn.

"Police recognize Crazy Cockroach, his henchbugs, and two new sidekicks wrapping the inn in toilet paper. From the logo on his brightly colored outfit, police believe one sidekick is called Furious Flea."

Eugene and Elle turned to each other and exclaimed, "Furious Flea!"

Eugene shook his head. "That has to be . . ."

Elle finished for him. "Fred!"

The Coolest Bug in School

Eugene and Elle weren't sure what to do. Should they call the cops and turn Fred in? Should they tattle to Fred's parents? Should they put on their superhero suits to confront all the villains at once?

Eugene said, "I don't want to get Fred in trouble."

Elle agreed. "We just want to pull him back to the good side of the diaper."

Eugene sighed. "Maybe if I'd spent more

time with him, this never would have happened."

Elle didn't want to make her big brother feel worse, so she stayed silent.

Eugene went on in a more hopeful tone. "I'll be extra nice to Fred tomorrow. That might help him come around."

Elle smiled. Who could possibly resist Eugene's charm?

The next day at school, Fred didn't just snub Eugene. He knocked the stack of books out of his former friend's arms, then laughed and stepped on his hands while Eugene struggled to retrieve them in the crowded hall.

"Hey, you missed your math book," Fred said. Then he scooped up the book and tossed it to Dee Dung.

Dee tossed the book to Doo, who tossed it to Cornelius, who tossed it back to Fred. It was a cruel game of Fly in the Middle.

Eugene held out his hand. Fred started to give Eugene the book, but at the last second he spit in the fly's hand instead.

The bully crew found this hysterically funny. In fact, they were so helpless with laughter that Eugene easily retrieved his math book. His dignity, however, remained on the dusty floor.

All day long, Eugene acted nice and Fred responded by being a total bad bug.

Cornelius saw great potential in this situation. He told his henchbugs, "This is the perfect setup for world domination!"

Dee and Doo looked blank. They had no idea what "domination" meant.

The super villain explained. "Now that Eugene and Fred are at odds, that means Super Fly and the flea formerly known as Fantastic Flea won't be working together to protect Stinkopolis and the rest of the world."

"Oh!" The dim Dungs were getting the idea.

Cornelius went on. "Let's widen the rift between fly and flea."

Again, "widen" and "rift" were hard words for his henchbugs to understand.

So Cornelius concluded, "Our mission is to make Fred Flea the coolest bug in school."

By the following day, all of Brown Barge Elementary School buzzed with praise for Fred Flea. No one could hop a dog like Fred. The amazing flea had once saved a centipede from choking on a maggot. Fred was great at sports, video games, circus tricks, and . . . everything!

By lunchtime Fred's legend went epic. Suddenly Fred Flea was everybug's hero, the bug everybug wanted to be. Fred ate surrounded by adoring fans offering him the best bites of their lunches.

Eugene sat in a quiet corner nibbling his deliciously disgusting lunch all by his lonesome.

Elle came up and said, "It's time Super Fly and Fly Girl had a talk with a certain flea."

Eugene sighed. "You're right."

10

The Dark Side of the Diaper

That night Stinkopolis suffered another crime spree. Crazy Cockroach, Furious Flea, Fiona, and the Dung twins wreaked havoc all over Chinatown.

The bad bugs tore down the strings of pretty lanterns, then emptied the garbage cans looking for tasty bits of moo shu poo and sweet-and-disgusting noodles.

All the while, Furious Flea ranted about his former friend. "Super Fly never uses his powers for fun. He's all about 'protecting the community' and 'saving the world.'" The flea popped a half-eaten dregs-roll in his mouth, then demanded, "Where's the fun in that?"

"None at all!" Crazy Cockroach exclaimed. "We should change his name from Super Fly to Pooper Fly—as in party pooper."

Furious Flea laughed. "Yeah, Mr. Super-Dooper Party Pooper practically faints every time he tries to talk to a pretty girl! And sometimes before a big test he gets so wound up he wets the bed. Maybe he should start wearing diapers instead of his Super Fly outfit," said the sarcastic flea. Every bug laughed. Even the Dungs got Fred's stupid joke.

Fred liked making his friends laugh, and he loved being the center of attention. So he continued trashing Super Fly. "And he's totally allergic to . . ."

Before Fred could reveal another of Super Fly's weaknesses, something *clinked* down the street. The roach and his hench-bugs went to investigate the sound.

As Fred started to follow, two figures suddenly stepped out of the shadows and grabbed him!

"Shh," someone hissed.

"We don't want to hurt you," a familiar voice said.

Fred suddenly recognized his attackers: Super Fly and Fly Girl!

"I'm sorry," Eugene began. "But I couldn't let you keep telling the enemy all my secrets! And by the way, I only wet my bed once and that's because it was a math test. You know how much I hate math."

Elle added, "We want the old Fred back—the good Fred, the one we like so much!"

But the flea felt way more Furious than Fantastic. Fred fumed, "I can't believe you two are lecturing me. **BUG OFF**!"

Elle and Eugene were too stunned to speak.

Fred ranted on. "Why don't you mind your own business? Being bad is way more fun than playing second fiddle—no, third fiddle—to a couple of houseflies. Fleas are cool too, and my new friends know that. Flies are boring. You're boring. Leave me alone."

Then Fred pushed his former friend so hard that Super Fly landed in a mud puddle! How could a Fantastic Flea push down a Super Fly? Fred's words had left Eugene feeling so confused that he literally became a pushover.

Eugene sputtered in the mud, flattened with disbelief. Did Fred really think Eugene considered fleas inferior? Had he somehow offended Fred?

Elle opened her mouth to protest, but Fred spoke first. "Your shoes and outfit are ugly!" the furious flea declared. "You look awful in that color." Then he hopped off into the night.

Super Fly and Fly Girl couldn't help but conclude that their friendship with the formerly fantastic flea was finished, donezo, over, kaput, history, buh-bye.

Crazy Cockroach, Number 1, and Number 2 quietly returned from the other end of the street to watch this sad scene. Of course to them it was a sweet victory.

Cornelius whispered to his henchbugs, "Let's go. Furious Flea can catch up with us later, in the dark side of the diaper."

Indeed, Fred soon found his new cohorts in the villain's cottony-soft lair. The flea asked, "Where've you been?"

Crazy Cockroach grinned. "Taking a dump."

Number 1 added, "Big dump."

Number 2 echoed, "Major!"

Then all three showed the flea the things they'd stolen from the dump. This certainly *was* major! In less than an hour the criminal crew had scooped up every toy, trinket, and snack Fred had ever wanted. "What am

I waiting for?" Furious Flea wondered. Why not pluck the poops of the world—or at least of Stinkopolis?

So he told Crazy Cockroach, "I want to take a dump too!"

The Dungs cheered. "All right, Furious Flea!"

Dee sang, "Who let the bad out?"

Doo waved the air in front of his nose and complained. "Seriously, who let the bad out?"

Fred blushed. "Sorry. I got excited."

Crazy Cockroach clapped him on the back and said, "Never be sorry. Be **BAD**!"

And with that the four bugs began a night of wicked fun.

11

Flies Flew Over the Cuckoo's Nest

Fred Flea had never felt so big before. Standing next to Fiona helped, because the female flea was even smaller than Fred.

But mostly, he felt big because lately every bug at Brown Barge treated him with respect. Being popular and cool was tons of fun! Way more fun than taking a backseat to a Super Nerd!

Fred convinced Cornelius and the Dung twins to form a quartet with him. Between classes the four bug buddies sang

in the halls. Everybug loved them!

Some tossed their lunch money at the singers. Others paid them in double-stuffed Poopios or other treats.

Fred felt like the King of the School, which was even better than Student of the Season. Bug butts moved aside as Fred walked down the halls. He was so cool they even seemed afraid, or at least terribly eager to please.

Fred's new pest friends wanted to play whatever game Fred suggested. And Fiona still laughed at Fred's jokes, even the dumb ones she'd heard before.

The other girl bugs also admired Fred.

Their eyes followed him wherever he went. Even Lucy Kaboosie wouldn't stop staring at the cool new Fred.

✻

Where was Eugene during all this? He was home from school feeling sick. Mrs. Flystein worried because she'd never seen her son so depressed before.

She presented Eugene with his favorite: chicken poop noodle soup.

Eugene didn't even have the energy to lift the spoon.

His mother put a cover on the steaming bowl. "Maybe later," she said as she left the room. "Try to rest."

The ripe aroma of genuine chicken poop simmered with all the right spices tempted Eugene. But he didn't think he deserved such a treat. Some genius he'd turned out to be.

He couldn't solve the invisibility problem, and, even worse, he couldn't come up with a way to fix things with Fred.

Elle felt depressed too. All her giggly friends noticed the little fly seemed to have lost her smile. A short time ago the second grader had been so cool. Now Elle dragged herself through the school day, her grades suffered, and she barely ate her lunch. She was still stunned by Fred's troubling transformation—and that really mean remark about her outfit and shoes! What do fleas know about color coordinating, anyway?

In the cafeteria, Elle heard cheering. She turned and saw Fred in the center of a crowd of adoring bugs. The athletic

flea was break dancing, which in Stinkopolis meant breaking things while dancing.

Fred twirled and leaped, tossing salt shakers at napkin holders. When a shaker smashed, scattering salt and glass everywhere, the crowd cheered even louder. Elle turned away in disgust.

When she got home, Elle found her brother standing in front of the open fridge mumbling to himself. And that wasn't the worst part: Eugene wore a dress—Elle's favorite dress! How he'd squeezed into it is another story.

12

Good Bugs Gone Bad

The next day, Mrs. Flystein made Eugene go to school. But he sulked and complained so much that soon no one wanted to have anything to do with the Student of the Season.

Lucy Kaboosie tried to cheer him up. "Things can't be that bad."

Eugene sighed. "The universe is a dark pit devoid of light. I'm the darkest part of that pit, and even the robot companion I built refuses to be friends with me."

It was Lucy's turn to sigh. "Maybe you just need to charge its battery."

"It's solar powered," Eugene mumbled.

Lucy walked away, shaking her head and muttering, "Or maybe you just need to stop feeling sorry for yourself."

Lucy wandered over to a swarm of bugs surrounding a mud puddle in front of Brown Barge. Elle stood at the edge of the group looking worried.

Lucy heard some voices from the swarm

saying things like, "It must be so cool to be bad!"

"Fred sure makes it look like fun!"

"I wish I could be as cool as Fred!"

Fiona's voice rose above the crowd. "Being bad *is* fun. Everything Fred does is cool. He's that kind of flea."

The swarm continued praising Fred.

"He's the greatest!"

"Fred is the new cool!"

"Bad is the new cool!"

"Cool is the new bad!"

Swarms never do make much sense. But when Elle heard a tiny moth declare, "I want to be bad when I grow up," her fists clenched with rage. Good bugs turning bad . . . that had to stop!

That night, Elle slipped out of her cozy pajamas to don the snazzy uniform of the flyest superhero, Fly Girl! When she reached in the drawer, Elle also found the tights Eugene had borrowed for his Super Fly costume.

Elle knew what that meant. No, her shy, thrifty brother had not bought his own pair of stretchy polyester tights. Eugene had given up!

Elle tied her shoes and then stood up. If Eugene wouldn't join her, the 9,000-times-enhanced second grader would face evil on her own.

Elle smiled down at her stylish shoes. They weren't ugly! Fred had only said that to hurt her feelings.

Elle's multifaceted eyes filled with tears. Why would dear, sweet Fred want to hurt her? Elle felt determined to find out!

So Fly Girl flew over the streets of

Stinkopolis, searching for the friend-turned-foe who had once been called Fantastic Flea. Wild whoops of nasty laughter drew Elle to an old trampoline in a shabby neighborhood.

"Check this out!" Dee Dung did a sloppy flip.

"No, this!" Doo shouted. His flip was even sloppier, leaving the dung beetle to scramble off his rounded back.

"That's nothing!" Crazy Cockroach performed a perfect double flip.

Then Furious Flea did a quadruple triple axel roundabout backflip, and the other bugs cheered!

A light snapped on in a nearby house, and then another and another. An angry voice demanded, "Don't you boys know what time it is?"

Crazy Cockroach cackled. "Time for fun!"

"If you don't quiet down I'm calling the cops!" another neighbor threatened.

Fred blew a raspberry and then shouted, "Go ahead and call!"

In seconds, Elle's super-hearing detected the first siren wailing toward the trampoline. She expected to see the bad boys scramble away. But they just kept bouncing and bragging, laughing even louder than before.

When the police arrived, one officer said, "Shouldn't you be in bed by now?"

His partner added, "It's a school night."

"School is for fools," Crazy Cockroach chanted, bouncing off the trampoline and onto the top of the police car.

Fred bounced from the trampoline onto the police car's hood. Then he and the roach flipped up in the air to land behind the officers.

When the police spun around to confront the bad boys, the flea and roach leaped back onto the trampoline, laughing in open defiance of both law and order!

The cops looked at each other and retreated to their car. Elle heard them calling for backup.

By the time they'd finished talking to the dispatcher, the bad boys had bounced away, still laughing at the top of their lungs.

Elle followed them down a dark street where they jumped a Best Pest Pizza delivery bug and stole his pooperoni pie!

Fred took a big, steaming bite. "Stolen pizza tastes even better than pizza you pay for."

Crazy Cockroach said, "I wouldn't know. I've never paid for a pizza before."

As the villains stuffed their mouths with pizza, Elle stepped out of the shadows and told Furious Flea, "I have something to show you."

Fred looked at the stretchy polyester tights neatly folded in her hands.

Elle asked, "Do you know what these are?"

Fred smiled. "Signs of a quitter!"

Elle couldn't hide her disappointment. She'd hoped that seeing part of Super Fly's costume would remind Fred of the noble purpose he'd shared with her brother.

But Furious Flea wasn't sentimental. In fact, he said, "I'm glad Super Fly gave up the superhero game! It'll save him the trouble of losing to me and my new buddies."

Number 1 added, "The stupid fly is no match for us."

Number 2 chimed in, "The only fly who's more of a loser is Fly Girl."

Elle didn't care what the Dungs thought. The musings of those microscopic brains meant nothing. But when Fred joined in the name-calling, that hurt! So she flew away before anyone could see her tears.

Furious Flea and his bully crew stayed out all night, making trouble all over Stinkopolis. At Brown Barge the next morning, they were exhausted wrecks. But they didn't care. School was just a place to nap, and to accept adoration and tribute from lesser bugs. Learning was for losers!

When some of the students wondered where Eugene was, Mrs. Tiger Moth said, "Eugene and his sister have the flu."

Dee burst out laughing. "Flies with the flu!"

Doo laughed too. "That's funny!"

At lunch, Cornelius told Fred something that was definitely not funny.

"Those tights last night, the flu this morning. Do you realize what this means?"

"Stretchy pants prevent you from getting sick?" replied Fred.

"No, flea brain!" continued Cornelius. "It means Super Fly is dead—or at least he might as well be. The only bug between world domination and us is Fly Girl. And she's just a little girl. Destroy Fly Girl, and we rule!"

Fiona liked the sound of that. "Awesome! I've always wanted to rule the world! The first rule I'm making is no more homework!"

The roach and his dumb beetles chuckled.

"How about no school at all?" suggested the wicked roach.

"Yes, even better!" Number 1 added.

"And no wearing pants!" Number 2 shouted.

The other villains stayed silent. They had no idea what Number 2 was talking about.

Then again, maybe that's why his name was Number 2.

Something in the back of Fred's mind protested. No, that didn't sound awesome. It was evil!

But Fred's busy jaws overruled his tired mind. All the desserts the adoring fans had heaped on Fred's tray made him woozy. The sugar high took the flea to a new low.

13

Rock 'Em, Sock 'Em

Mr. Flystein, an inventor like his son, Eugene, often became lost in his work. Yet even he noticed when a week passed and Eugene kept wearing the same stained jeans and sweaty T-shirt. The normally stylish Elle looked even worse! Sleepless for a week, the second grader looked more like a zombie than a secret superhero. The stress was definitely taking its toll on the Flystein siblings.

Mrs. Flystein cooked the kids' favorite breakfast: rotten eggs and decaying bacon drizzled in poop. Not even when they really had the flu had her young ever looked so flat. They needed a boost!

The Flystein siblings sat together on the bus to Brown Barge. Cornelius spat spitballs at them while Fred, Fiona, and the Dungs laughed.

They'd had enough. Hot anger burned the fog from Elle's brain. Eugene felt the same burst of energy. The siblings suddenly knew the only way to snap Fred out of his bad-bug craze would be an old-fashioned bug butt-kicking. Super Fly and Fly Girl were just the ones to do it!

As soon as they stepped off the bus, Eugene confronted Fred. "You're not a bad bug. And I'm going to prove that to you!"

"Your days of telling me who I am and what to do are over!" Furious Fred shouted back. The flea flexed his impressive muscles. Fred was small, but he really was furious!

"You couldn't hurt a fly even if you tried," said Eugene.

"Oh yeah? Try me, Flystein!" replied Fred.

Eugene knew that as Super Fly he could easily beat his former pest friend. He didn't want to hurt Fred. But . . .

Fred bounced toward Eugene. One fist swooped past Eugene's face. The fly felt the breeze from the blow, which would've been a doozy. Furious Fred laughed. "I'll handle you after school!"

Then the bell rang and the crowd scrambled into the building. Elle didn't see Fred again until lunch.

The spunky second grader told Fred exactly what she thought of him. "You used to be so cool. Now you think you're cool, but you're just mean and stupid."

Then she turned to Fiona. "And you're mean and stupid too! Or you'd know the best things about Fred aren't how bad he is, but how kind and talented and . . ."

Fiona stuck a finger down her throat and pretended to puke. "You flies make me sick. After school I'll show you that fleas rule!"

Grime-flavored gelatin was the dessert of the day. The lunchtime gossip focused on the big fight scheduled for the final bell. It was a "Flies versus Fleas" showdown.

But when fight time finally came, Elle and Eugene were nowhere to be found. Then the sky buzzed with the sound of super-fast wings. The students of Brown Barge looked up in amazement as Super Fly and Fly Girl looped and swooped through the air, putting on a display of aerial artistry worthy of the Insect Corps' elite air squadron, the Bug Angels.

The crowd oohed and aahed in time to the dazzling flight of the super flies!

The students quickly forgot about the fight in favor of this awesome spectacle in the sky.

Fred became furious! He refused to let the Flystein duo deprive him of the battle he craved. Fred told Cornelius, Dee, and Doo, "Tonight will be the showdown: Good versus Bad; Super Fly versus Furious Flea!"

Cornelius couldn't have been happier if he'd found a polluted river of french fry grease. These events fell right into place with his evil plan. By that night, the bug robot army he'd been building on his side of the dirty diaper would be ready. As soon as Furious Flea started playing rock 'em, sock 'em with Super Fly . . .

14

Super Fleas

Eugene and Elle suspected that Crazy Cockroach was up to something. After all, the mean roach wasn't friends with Fred because he enjoyed his company. Not that Fred's company wasn't enjoyable, but evil was a habit with bullies like Cornelius. Being enhanced 9,000 times just meant he bullied on a bigger scale.

Brother and sister had finished their after-school snack, so they moved from the Flystein kitchen to the living room. Elle flopped on the couch. Eugene paced back and forth, as he often did when he was thinking.

Eugene guessed, "Cornelius is probably building a bug robot army or something to take over the world."

Elle agreed. "He's not the type to be practicing his Ping-Pong game or reading the classics."

Eugene laughed, recalling his triumph at

Ping-Pong in the villain's lair. But could he count on beating Crazy Cockroach again? This time Eugene didn't even know the villain's game. He mused, "We need to somehow trick Cornelius into revealing his plan."

Elle added, "Once he does, Fred's bound to realize the roach has just been using him, and his new 'friends' weren't really his friends at all."

Eugene smiled for the first time in a long time as he told his sister, "I hope you're right!"

So the super siblings put their heads together to plan their strategy for the fight against Furious Flea and Fiona.

Eugene said, "Maybe we should pretend the fleas are beating us. That will make Crazy Cockroach feel confident. Villains can't resist the urge to gloat and spill the beans, especially if they feel sure they're going to win."

"Are you saying give fleas a chance?" said Elle.

"That's exactly what I'm saying," said Eugene.

Elle knew where her brother was going. "Once Crazy Cockroach declares his plan for world domination, Furious Flea will finally understand what's happening."

At that very moment, Fred slinked past the talking flies unseen. He wasn't listening to their conversation. Fred was intent upon his goal: the slice of the Ultimo 6-9000 in the Flysteins' fridge. That pastry would give him the power to defeat Super Fly!

Fred knew it was wrong to steal, especially from someone who until recently had been his pest friend. But he couldn't resist the temptation to become 9,000 times faster, better, stronger, cooler.

So Fred eased open the refrigerator door and snuck a bite of the oozy, yellowish-green pie. He broke off another chunk to take with him.

The ooze tasted nothing like he expected, more like wet cardboard than key lime. But Fred didn't care about taste; he wanted the pie's powers!

Then the sneaky flea quietly closed the refrigerator door and . . .

Six seconds had elapsed since the pie arrived in Fred's stomach. The flea felt a surge of energy, power, and strength! He bounced, and the force of it bounced Fred right through the Flysteins' ceiling.

Oops! So much for stealth mode. Fred chuckled to himself. He felt super fantastic. Fantastic Flea. No, not anymore, no one's sidekick. He was Furious Flea, and he was going to kick Super Fly's nerdy butt once and for all.

Fred cradled the precious bit of lime pie in his hand. Fiona would be so pleased! Didn't his special new friend deserve to be super too? Together they'd be fleas of great force, respected and feared. *Fearless Fiona has a nice ring to it,* Fred thought as he soared through the sky.

*

Fred wasn't the only bad boy gloating in evil glee. At that very moment in his stained and stinking lair, Crazy Cockroach tightened the final bolt on the last bug robot in his army of 1,001 robots. Armed and obedient to any command, the robots stood ready to play their part in the insane insect's scheme to take over the world.

Cornelius savored the sweet anticipation of victory. This time he would win! Super Fly couldn't possibly defeat him. Not with his new fleamates. The hapless hero would be too busy defending himself against his own pest friend!

Crazy Cockroach burst into laughter so violent he almost choked. "Phew! Funny. Almost died there. Died laughing? That would be funny. But no, I have better things to do. This is going to be the best night of my life!"

The roach gloated. "Tonight I'll watch my enemies fight. And while they're distracted in the heat of battle, beating each other up, I, Crazy Cockroach, will take over the world!"

The villain cackled. "I am *such* a genius!"

15

Fly vs. Flea

Stinkopolis stank that night, even worse than usual. The town reeked with the smell of crime, in this case the senseless destruction of public property.

Crazy Cockroach and his henchbugs had stolen someone's golf bag. So they each swung a club, trying to swat the dimpled balls into the windows of Brown Barge Elementary School.

Number 1 missed the ball completely.

So did Number 2. "No wonder everybug complains about this game. It's harder than it looks!"

Their 9,000-times-enhanced companion swung his club at the tiny target. The white ball sailed toward the school. Then with a loud *crash* it smashed right through one of the windows!

Numbers 1 and 2 cheered.

Cornelius cackled. "He shoots! He scores!"

Then he placed another ball on the ground, swung the club and . . . **CRASH**! Another of the school's windows landed in shards on the muddy ground. This continued for another 547 golf balls smashing into windows. Yes, the school has a lot of windows, thanks for noticing.

Super Fly felt a rush of anger. What kind of jerk wrecks his own school? This Crazy Cockroach had to be stopped!

So Super Fly and Fly Girl rushed to take on the evil cockroach and his criminal cohorts.

Super Fly buzzed toward the roach so fast all Numbers 1 and 2 saw was a blur.

Super Fly's fist crashed into Crazy Cockroach's jaw with a **CRACK** as loud as a baseball bat hitting a home run.

But the 9,000-times-enhanced villain wasn't even fazed by this tremendous blow! Instead, he countered with an equally hard slam at Super Fly's shoulder. The hit nearly knocked Super Fly beyond the borders of Stinkopolis!

Meanwhile, Fly Girl battled the Dungs. The nasty beetles were nearly twice the second grader's size. But they didn't pull any punches against the girl.

Number 1 and Number 2 swung their fists as hard as they could. A left from Dee and a right from Doo, another left, another right. The punches fell so fast that even the enhanced superhero couldn't evade them all.

Fly Girl exclaimed, "Ow!"

Dee laughed cruelly.

"Ooof!" she shouted as another punch connected with her kidney.

Rage added strength to Elle's counterpunch, and Dee went flying right into Brown Barge's flagpole. He landed on his hard, rounded back and quickly returned to the battle.

Just then, Fly Girl recognized two new

arrivals: Furious Flea and Fiona. The female flea sneered at Fly Girl. "Hello, ugly shoes. Are you ready to rumble?"

Fly Girl didn't know both fleas had tasted the key-lime-flavored enhancer. She soon got her first clue.

"You can call me Fearless Fiona," the girl flea announced. Then her eyes narrowed with menace. "Or you could just call me your worst nightmare!"

Then she slapped Fly Girl so hard that the young superhero flew into the air faster than if she'd been shot from a cannon. Elle gasped in disbelief.

At the same time, Furious

Flea joined Crazy Cockroach's epic struggle against Super Fly. With one amazingly powerful punch, Furious Flea sent Super Fly skidding across the school yard on his back. Broken glass from the shattered windows tore at Super Fly's wings.

Furious Flea didn't wait for Super Fly to stand up. Instead, he and Crazy Cockroach started punching as fast as their enhanced muscles allowed. This was even faster than the poor fly could exclaim, "Ouch! Hey! Wait a second!"

The brilliant brains of both Flystein heroes reached the same conclusion at the same time: the fleas had somehow tasted the Ultimo 6-9000. To their horror, the super siblings also realized they no longer needed to *pretend* they were getting their butts kicked.

Fly Girl groaned. "Uh-oh!"

Super Fly whispered, "We're getting our butts kicked—for real!"

Super Fly tried to reason with his former friend. But Furious Flea remained furious!

Between blows, Fly Girl tried talking to Fiona. But Fearless Fiona wasn't exactly the let's-be-reasonable type.

So the battle raged on. Super bug versus equally super bug; punches and kicks, pinches and slaps, wrestling holds and school yard tricks; even some biting (that's what fleas do). There was scratching, poking, noogies, headlocks, and hair pulling; all adding up to an amazing contest where victory and defeat changed sides too often for anyone to keep track.

Then suddenly the skies over Stinkopolis darkened with the arrival of 1,001 flying robot bugs! This time the super siblings both exclaimed at the same time, "**WHAT THE** . . . ?"

At that very moment their newly enhanced former flea friend suddenly perceived the truth: this *was* all a setup! Lucy Kaboosie was right. His new "friends" had lured him into a trap. Everything had been part of another insane scheme to take over Stinkopolis! How could I be so stupid? Fred thought miserably.

The roach reveled in his own brilliance. Victory would soon be his. Stinkopolis and then the whole world would be at his feet. Odds clearly favored him. What hope could two flies, even super flies, have against a 1,001-robot army?

However, the odds turned out to be a little odder than Crazy Cockroach calculated. Since he hadn't planned on Furious Flea eating the Ultimo 6-9000 and giving some to Fiona.

Suddenly both super fleas sprang into furious action against the robots. Fearless Fiona joined the fight because she was sweet on Fred and because, with enhanced strength, fighting robots was even more fun than sneaking into the movies.

Cornelius felt confused. How could an ordinary flea punch a robot into a heap of twisted metal—or stomp another as flat as a crushed soda can?

Of course, the 9,000-times-smarter roach quickly reasoned that the fleas must've tasted the Dessert of Destiny. But what could he do about that? Nothing, except watch the four super bugs defeat his entire robot army in less than fifteen minutes (or 900 seconds, for those who prefer smaller time measurements)!

16

Fearless or Fabulous?

Soon super-strong rope (another of Eugene's successful inventions) bound Crazy Cockroach to his henchbugs. The roach brooded over his latest defeat. He should be  ruler of the world by now! Why was he tied to these dumb Dungs?

Meanwhile, the conversation between Fantastic Flea, Super Fly, and Fly Girl made the frustrated villain feel downright disgusted.

"I'm sorry I took your friendship for granted," Super Fly told Fred.

"I'm sorry I fell for Cornelius's crackpot scheme," Fred echoed.

"I'm sorry I didn't pay closer attention to both of you," Elle added. "Friends should watch each other's backs. And sometimes wash each other's backs, if they land in sticky stuff."

The three good bugs moved in for a hug. Fred kept one arm open to welcome Fiona. But the pretty flea shook her head. "I'm not like you," she began. "I'm Fearless Fiona!"

Fred didn't understand. "That's just a name, like Furious or Fantastic Flea. You can change your name to something more positive. Fabulous Fiona, Friendly, or whatever."

"That's right," Elle chimed in. "It doesn't even have to start with an F. Maybe you could be Super Flea or Flea Girl."

Fiona laughed harshly. "Save that corny sap for each other. I enjoy being a bad bug—and I kind of like the idea of the world being run by bad bugs."

Fred sighed. Fiona was so much fun. Could she really be . . . evil?

Apparently so, because the moment the three good bugs flew away, Fearless Fiona untied Crazy Cockroach and his mean-spirited minions. She even helped them pick up all the broken robot parts scattered around Brown Barge Elementary.

Crazy Cockroach shrugged. He hated

defeat. But tomorrow was another day, and another chance to rule the world.

He may have lost his 1,001-robot army, but at least he'd gained a pretty, superpowered, evil flea.

Tomorrow was a new day for the good bugs too. Fred and Eugene were glad to be back together as pest friends. Elle's giggly gang enjoyed seeing her back to her smiling, super-cool self.

Cornelius and the Dungs didn't bother coming to school. They had bruises to nurse and new devious plans to make. Nobody missed them, not even Mrs. Tiger Moth, who preferred a spitball-free classroom.

As for Fiona, she went to school. She was even nice to Fred. Because although she was bad and he preferred being good, Fiona still liked Fred.

And that could lead to trouble.

Todd H. Doodler is the author and illustrator of the Super Fly series, *Rawr!* and the Bear in Underwear series, as well as many other fun books for young readers. He is also the founder of David & Goliath, a humorous T-shirt company, and Tighty Whitey Toys, which makes plush animals in underwear. He, too, is a part-time superhero and lives in Los Angeles with his daughter, Elle, and their two labradoodles, Muppet and Pickleberry.